King and C

# The King
# at Christmas

by Allen Saddler

*Illustrated by Joe Wright*

Oxford University Press 1983

*Oxford   Toronto   Melbourne*

Oxford University Press, Walton Street, Oxford OX2 6DP

Oxford  London  Glasgow
New York  Toronto  Melbourne  Auckland
Kuala Lumpur  Singapore  Hong Kong  Tokyo
Delhi  Bombay  Calcutta  Madras  Karachi
Nairobi  Dar es Salaam  Cape Town

and associated companies in
Beirut  Berlin  Ibadan  Mexico City  Nicosia

*Oxford* is a trade mark of Oxford University Press

*British Library Cataloguing in Publication Data*
Saddler, Allen
The King at Christmas.—(King & Queen Book)
I. Title
823'.914[J]  PZ7
ISBN 0-19-279775-1

Photoset in Great Britain by
Rowland Phototypesetting Ltd, Bury St Edmunds, Suffolk
and printed in Hong Kong

*P*
75536

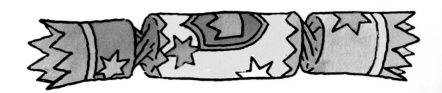

On Christmas Eve the King stared out of the window.

'I expect it will snow,' he said. 'It usually does.'

On the Palace Green a group of carol singers walked into view, carrying a lantern.

'Quick,' said the King. 'Give them some money, or they'll start singing.'

The King opened the window and threw out some pennies.

'Thank you,' said the head carol singer. 'Which carol would you like?'

'I don't want any,' said the King. 'I heard them all last year.'

'Don't be such a misery,' said the Queen. 'You can't have carol singers if they don't sing any carols.'

'Oh, all right,' said the King. 'Just a quick one.'

The King climbed onto his second best throne and put his hands over his ears.

'I suppose we'll get turkey again tomorrow,' he said.

'Of course it's turkey,' said the Queen. 'You always have turkey at Christmas.'

'I don't see why,' said the King. 'We had turkey last year. What about a kipper, or soft roes on toast?'

'You can't carve a kipper,' said the Queen. 'There's not enough to go round.'

The carol singers stopped and the King went over to the window.

'Good bye,' he shouted. 'See you next year.'

The head carol singer bowed low.
'It will be our pleasure,' he said.
'It won't be mine,' said the King,
shutting the window.

The Royal Magician entered and bowed so low that his hat tipped off.

'I was wondering whether you might like something special for tomorrow?'

'Yes,' said the King. 'Could you put it off for a few weeks? All the Palace servants expect an extra day off, and it messes everything up.'

No dinner today having a day off. Signed Cook

The Magician looked worried.

'Your wish is my command,' he said. 'But I cannot alter the moon and the sun, or the calendar.'

'Not much of a magician are you,' said the King, 'if you can't do a simple thing like that. We'll have to get extra servants in, and pay them.'

'What about some snow?' said the Magician. 'I might be able to manage that.'

'Oh no,' said the King. 'We'd have to get people to shovel and sweep it away.'

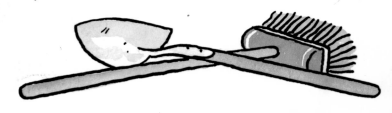

The King walked down the Royal passage, which was lit up with coloured lights. At the end of the passage the Royal Christmas tree was covered in coloured balls, tinsel and small parcels.

The King marched back to the Queen.

'Look,' he said. 'Can't we just have the presents? We could have a cracker and some jelly. Then it would be all over.'

'What about the party?' said the Queen.

'What party?' said the King.

'The Christmas party,' said the Queen. 'The Princess has invited twenty guests. And my sister is coming with her children.'

'Twenty guests!' said the King. 'Have we got to feed all that lot? We'll be having bread and water until Easter.'

The next morning the King went onto the Palace balcony to wave to the crowd. The people cheered and shouted 'Merry Christmas!'

'Is it?' said the King, as he marched back inside.

The Court Jester asked the King to pull a cracker.

'No thanks,' said the King. 'They make a noise. I'll have a mince pie.'

'They're not ready yet,' said the Queen. 'The cook has just put them in the oven.'

The King walked along to the Royal banqueting hall, where the banqueting maids were laying the table.

'Turkey, I suppose,' said the King.

'Yes,' said the Head Royal Butler, 'and stuffing.'

'Sprouts?' said the King.

'Oh yes,' said the Head Royal Butler, 'and carrots, cabbage and boiled beans.'

'That settles it,' said the King. 'I hate sprouts and cabbage and boiled beans. Where's that magician?'

The Royal Magician hurried into the hall and bowed low.

'About this snow,' said the King. 'Could you get a lot of it? I mean, enough to block up the roads? There's about fifty people coming to dinner. They'll all want to play games and make a noise. And they'll all be eating and drinking.'

'Would you like a small snow storm?' said the Magician.

'What about a blizzard?' said the King, 'but be quick about it. They'll be setting off soon.'

'Your wish is my command,' said the Magician.

Suddenly the sky went black. The snow started to fall, swirling around the Palace and piling up in heavy drifts. The King looked out of the window, rubbing his hands with glee.

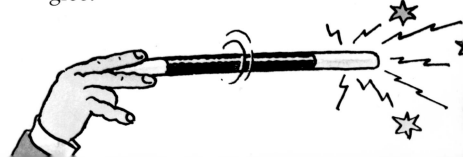

'There's too much there to get shovelled away,' he said. 'We'll put off the Christmas Party. We'll have it at Easter.'

The wind blew hard along the Royal passage, and all the lights went out.

'OOoo,' said the King. 'I can't see.'

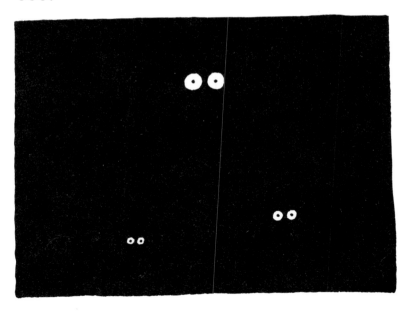

The King held onto the passage wall and crept slowly back to the Queen.

'Sorry about the party,' he said. 'Nobody will set out in this. What about a mince pie?'

'Mince pie!' said the Queen. 'There'll be no mince pies today. The oven has gone off, so we can't cook anything.'

'What,' said the King, 'no turkey, no sprouts, cabbage or boiled beans?'

'There'll be no dinner at all,' said the Queen, 'if we can't cook it.'

The snow kept falling thick and heavy, piling up the steps to the Palace.

'What a shame!' said the Queen. 'All the party guests will be disappointed. And they were all bringing presents.'

'Presents?' said the King. 'Presents for me?'

'Of course,' said the Queen. 'People always bring presents at Christmas.'

The King stared out of the window, feeling hungry.

'I knew it would snow,' he said. 'It always does.'